Nuts

NOEL FORD

PUFFIN BOOKS

PUFFIN BOOKS

Published by the Penguin Group
Penguin Books Ltd, 27 Wrights Lane, London W8 5TZ, England
Penguin Books USA Inc., 375 Hudson Street, New York, New York 10014, USA
Penguin Books Australia Ltd, Ringwood, Victoria, Australia
Penguin Books Canada Ltd, 10 Alcorn Avenue, Toronto, Ontario, Canada M4V 3B2
Penguin Books (NZ) Ltd, 182–190 Wairau Road, Auckland 10, New Zealand

Penguin Books Ltd, Registered Offices: Harmondsworth, Middlesex, England

First published by Viking 1991
Published in Puffin Books 1992
10 9 8 7 6 5 4 3 2 1

Printed in England by Clays Ltd, St Ives plc
Filmset in Linotron Palatino

Contents

1
Saved by Miss Bell

Billy Thomas Lowe was quite small for a nine-year-old – Lowe by name and low by nature, his parents joked – but he had a BIG secret. It was a secret for which the brainiest scientists in the land would give their electron microscopes. Still, he thought to himself, I've promised not to tell *them* so I'm certainly not going to tell Barrie Barns.

Unfortunately, it was beginning to look as if he wasn't going to have much choice in the matter. His short legs, which had initially given him a good start on the bigger boy, were tiring. His chest ached, and he was finding it more and more difficult to keep running. The things he was carrying didn't help matters either.

"Come here, Beetle! I only want to talk to you!"

That was another thing Billy didn't like about his name. Those initials. B.T.L. Nearly everyone , including some of his teachers, called him Beetle.

"Don't be frightened! Really, I only want to talk!" Barrie's voice was louder now. Was he just shouting more loudly or was he catching up? Billy, still running as fast as he could, looked over his shoulder. He knew what Barrie's "talks" were like. The last time the two of them had had a "talk", Billy had finished the conversation with a tooth missing.

"Stop!"

It only took a second for Billy to realize that the command had come, not from behind but from in front of him. It was a second too long. With a crash he hurtled into the newspaper stand on the street corner. Copies of the lunch-time edition flew everywhere; into the road, over the pavement, over the newspaper seller who had shouted the warning and over Billy who lay sprawled on the ground, badly winded from the collision.

Words drifted before his eyes. **Supermarket Snatcher Strikes Again**. He realized that the words were the headline on a newspaper, lying on the pavement in front of him. He didn't stop to read any more, though. Gasping for breath he staggered to his feet, still, amazingly, clutching his precious possessions.

And then he felt a hand gripping him under his arm.

"Come on, Beetle. On your feet."

Barrie Barns! Billy felt his arm

THE TEMPLEBAY TRUMPET
SUPERMARKET SNATCHER STRIKES AGAIN

beginning to go numb from Barrie's tight grip.

"Just a minute, you two." The newspaper seller! Now it was Barrie's turn to feel his arm going numb as the angry man grabbed him tightly. Startled, he relaxed his grip on Billy and the smaller boy snatched away from him and was off, down the road.

"Hey, you! Come back here!" The newspaper man shouted in vain. Barrie took advantage of the man's distraction and, pulling his own arm free, ran after Billy. The chase was on again.

Weaving his way through lunch-time shoppers, his arms aching from the weight of the things he was carrying, Billy made for the alley. It was his only chance. If he could dash down there without Barrie seeing him, he could make good his escape.

A few more breathless steps and – he was there. Now down the alley. Past the point where it narrowed before turning and joining the next street.

"Oh no!" He felt the disappointment flow down to his knees, taking all the strength from them. Rounding the corner, he was faced by a large builder's rubbish skip, completely blocking his path. Worse, from around the corner behind him came the sound of running feet. He was trapped.

"Right then, Beetle. Just what *is* this?" Barrie was leafing through the battered old book which he had snatched from Billy's trembling hand. The book which, twenty minutes ago, he had watched Billy take from the biscuit tin down on the beach.

"Give it back to me, Barrie, it's not mine," Billy pleaded, but Barrie Barns continued to turn the pages while Billy, tears forming in his eyes and his fair hair dripping with perspiration, stood looking up at him. In his right hand he still clutched the treasured metal detector that his mum and dad had given him last birthday.

Barrie laughed. "Well, I know it's not yours. I saw you dig it up from the sand, down by old Hammy's place. Besides, it's all in some foreign language. Not proper writing at all, just these weird squiggles. More likely belongs to a martian than you, Beetle. You're not a martian, are you?"

"Please give it back, I really need it. Look – you can borrow my metal detector for a week – a month!" The tears were very close now, and Billy made a big effort to hold them back. He was angry with himself, too, for letting Barrie think that the book was important.

"I've got a metal detector. Better than that rubbish you've got there," Barrie sneered. That was true. His parents had bought him the top model in the range and he had used it for a whole morning before getting bored with it.

"Anyway, if this book's so important, perhaps I ought to hang on to it." As he spoke, some loose pages fell from the back of the book. He bent down to pick them up but Billy was too quick for him and was down on his knees scooping them up. Barrie dropped down to his own knees and grabbed the

pages but Billy held on tightly.

"Hello, you two, what's going on then? Barrie Barns! Not bullying young Beetle here, I hope?"

The voice of Miss Bell, the music teacher at Templebay Junior School, struck dismay and joy, respectively, into the hearts of Barrie and Billy. Barrie had his mouth open to protest his innocence but before his brain could come up with a believable story to pass on to his tongue, Billy was speaking.

"No, Miss, it's all right. I dropped my book and papers and Barrie was helping me to pick them up. Thanks, Barrie." He took the book and papers from Barrie's unresisting hands. Miss Bell looked pleasantly, if a little doubtfully, surprised.

"Well now, Barrie," she said. "Are you sure you're feeling well? Not been out in this unexpected sunshine too long, have we?" Barrie definitely *wasn't* feeling well but he could hardly tell Miss Bell why.

"No, Miss," he mumbled.

"Well then, perhaps this new Barrie Barns, the one who wants to help people, would like to tell me what he's going to be doing for the school Charity Day next Friday?" Miss Bell turned to

Billy. "You run along, Beetle. Barrie can walk along with me for a while and tell me how he's going to help raise money for the Guide Dogs. You don't mind, do you Barrie? Keeping me company on the way to the school?"

Billy said goodbye to Miss Bell and gratefully ran off clasping the book and loose papers in one hand and his metal detector in the other. He smiled to himself. Miss Bell was no fool. She hadn't believed a word of what he'd said about Barrie helping him. She was just giving him time to get safely away.

It was only much later that a thought occurred to him. Why was Miss Bell walking down the alley if she was on her way to school, which lay in the opposite direction?

2
A Hamster in Paradise

Billy arrived at the pet shop just in time. It was five minutes to two and Pets' Paradise was one of the few shops in Templebay that still closed on Monday afternoons.

"Hello, lad," Mr Harris, the owner greeted him. "Been treasure hunting, have we?" Billy was puzzled for a moment but then remembered he was still carrying the metal detector.

"What? Oh – yes. No luck though. Just a few tin cans and things. Have you still got Mr – er– the hamster?" Billy had almost said, "Have you still got Mr Hammond?" but that would never do. How could he possibly explain to Mr

PUSSDINS
HAPPY WAGGERS DOG BISCUITS
Pets' Paradise

Harris that the hamster which Barrie Barns and his pal, Nosy, had brought into the shop last Wednesday was really Mr Hammond, a teacher at his school?

He could hardly believe it himself. Could it be that he had dreamed the whole thing? Dreamed that, only two days ago, in this very shop, a hamster had quietly spoken to him of a magical experiment that had gone woefully wrong? If it *had* been a dream, though, how come he had found the book? The book which, hopefully, would put things right and which he had found buried down at the beach just as the hamster claiming to be Mr Hammond had told him?

"The hamster?" Mr Harris exclaimed, jolting Billy back to the present. "Of course I have. I promised to keep him for you, didn't I? He's over there. Still in the same place." Then the shopkeeper seemed to think of something and looked at Billy severely. "Here," he said, sharply, "shouldn't you be at school now?"

"No. Day off, Mr Harris. Only the teachers are in today. Something to do with special training."

Mr Harris raised his eyebrows. They were big and bushy, in contrast to his shiny pink bald head. They were so hairy that some of the children from school reckoned he was trying to grow them long enough to comb back and replace the hair which had long since deserted him. "Well, there's a turn up," he said. "Teachers having to go back to school, eh?" He chuckled at the thought.

Billy was already heading for the corner of the shop where Mr Harris kept the mice, gerbils, guinea-pigs and hamsters. Pets' Paradise was aptly named. As well as these small rodents, Mr Harris had puppies, kittens, rabbits, fish and a large blue and yellow parrot named Charlie who could recite everything from the twelve-times table to the names of the entire Manchester United football team. Normally Billy would stop for a chat with Charlie but today he headed straight for the hamsters.

Sure enough, it was still there, just as Mr Harris had promised. There were about a dozen of them in the cage but the

one that Billy wanted was keeping to itself, well away from the others.

"Unsociable little beast, isn't he?" Mr Harris had joined Billy at the cage. "Been like that all weekend. Refuses to have anything to do with the others. Are you sure that's the one you want?"

"Oh yes. Absolutely."

"Right, come here then." Mr Harris opened the cage and reached inside. Quick as a flash, Billy's hamster leapt on to Mr Harris's hand, ran up his arm, on to his head, skidding a little on the shiny surface, then down his other arm and *plop*! straight into the little cardboard box which the astonished shopkeeper had brought over with him.

"Well, I'll be. . . !" Mr Harris looked at the box in his left hand in amazement. "I've never seen anything like it. Almost as if he *wanted* to go with you."

"Rubbish!" a voice cackled in the background. Mr Harris ignored the remark. It was only Charlie, who was feeling a bit neglected. He was the star of the pet shop and he didn't take too kindly to being upstaged by a ridiculous little hamster.

They were back at the counter and Mr Harris had sealed the box, making sure the air-holes were clear. "I'll give you some food to start you off. I suppose you'll be needing a cage, too, and a little wheel, perhaps?"

"Er . . . no thanks. I've got them already, at home," Billy said quickly, blushing as he spoke the lie. These were the last things this hamster would want, though the thought of Mr Hammond trotting merrily in his little wheel almost made him laugh out loud. "Just the hamster, please."

Having paid, he left the shop. Charlie called out, "You'll be sorrrreeee!" but Billy took no notice and hurried down the street and around the corner.

Mr Harris had given him a carrier bag to carry the box, the hamster food and the book in. As Billy passed a litter bin he took the hamster food from the carrier bag and dropped it into the bin. Ordinary hamster food was not going to do Mr Hammond much good. He had already bought the right food before going to the pet shop – the food which Mr Hammond had insisted on.

Things were starting to go right again, now. He had the book, he had the hamster and, in his pocket, he had the food. A small bag full of hazel-nuts.

Half an hour later, Billy arrived at The Old Boathouse, an ancient weatherbeaten building which Mr

Hammond, "Old Hammy", as the children at Billy's school called him, had converted into a ramshackle sort of house. Although it was the middle of November there were quite a few people on the beach, taking advantage of the unusually mild sunny weather.

Billy climbed the rickety steps and turned the handle of Mr Hammond's front (and only!) door. Just as the hamster had told him, it wasn't locked. The door swung open.

Inside, he marvelled at the delightful confusion. The bookshelves were crammed to overflowing and those books for which there was no room were piled everywhere; on the chairs, the table, the floor – even on the side of the sink where they had to share the space with several days worth of unwashed plates and chemistry equipment.

In one corner of the room, a video camera stood on its tripod, like an oil rig in a sea of books. As he looked at the camera, a shrill whistle drew Billy's attention to the opposite corner which was occupied by a large brass bird cage. From its perch, a bright yellow canary returned his gaze.

"That's Chips, the cause of all the trouble," said a muffled voice from the box in Billy's carrier bag. "You'll find some bird seed in the cupboard under the sink and you'd better top up his water. But first, if you don't mind, get me out of here."

Billy put down his metal detector, moved a pile of books from an armchair, sat down and placed the carrier bag on his lap. From it, he took the book and the box containing the hamster. He then opened the box and placed it on top of

the small pile of books on the table beside the chair.

From the open end of the box a twitching nose appeared, followed by the rest of the odd little hamster. Twitching its whiskers, it looked around the room and then, giving Billy a quizzical look said, "Well done, Billy. Well done indeed. And the book?"

"Yes, I've got the book," Billy replied. "And I haven't told anyone. Just like I promised you in the pet shop, on Saturday."

"Good boy. I knew I could trust you." The hamster looked pleased.

"You really *are* Old Hammy – er – I mean, Mr Hammond, aren't you? I mean, I'm not just dreaming this?" Billy said.

"No, Billy," the hamster/Mr Hammond replied. "You're not

dreaming it, although, for me, you'll understand, it is rather a nightmare."

Billy was sorry for Mr Hammond, of course, but he was curious, too. "Hammy – sorry – Mr Hammond . . ."

"That's all right Billy. I think 'Hammy' is rather appropriate, don't you?" Mr Hammond chuckled, his whiskers twitching again.

"Well, yes, I . . . well, what I mean is . . . sir, can you tell me what exactly happened to you?"

The hamster grew suddenly serious.

"Yes, yes, of course, Billy. If you're going to help me, you must know everything. But first things first. You've got the book but did you remember the nuts? I have to get started on the nuts. There's so little time, you see."

3
The Practical Wizard's Do-It-Yourself Handbook

While Billy fed Chips, the canary, Mr Hammond, the teacher who had somehow been turned into a hamster, munched hungrily on the hazel-nuts.

Buying the pound of nuts and the hamster had taken every last penny of the pocket money that Billy's parents gave to him every Monday. Still, it was worth it. Nothing like this had ever happened to him before.

When Billy returned to the armchair, Mr Hammond was just stuffing the last six nuts into his cheek pouches. He cleared his throat, wiped his mouth with both paws and, as soon as Billy was seated, began his story.

"First of all, Billy, you truly have to believe who I am. Wait!" Mr Hammond held up a paw to stop Billy from interrupting. "I know you *think* you believe me but it's really important that, deep, deep down, you don't have a single doubt."

"But I do believe, sir, really I do," Billy protested. "Once I realized, last Saturday in Pets' Paradise that a hamster was talking to me, it was hardly any bother at all believing it was you."

"I suppose," Mr Hammond said stiffly, his little nose quivering, "you thought that if such a thing could happen at all, it could only happen to an old crackpot like Hammy."

"Well . . ."

"It's all right, Billy. I know what people say behind my back. Everyone thinks I'm a little strange. I'll bet no one at school is the slightest bit concerned that I haven't been there since last Tuesday."

This was true. Mr Hammond's eccentric ways were well known to the staff of Templebay Junior. It was quite normal for him to disappear for two or three days and then turn up as if nothing had happened.

"Anyway, as I was saying, it's most important that you believe that I am who I claim to be. Because, if you can, then it's just possible that you'll believe what I'm going to tell you now."

So Billy listened, ready to believe the unbelievable.

"It was last Tuesday night. I'd finally managed to translate some of the pages of the book which, thankfully, you have managed to recover for me. I was making my notes when . . ." Mr Hammond stopped abruptly and then asked, anxiously, "The notes? You did find the notes, too?"

"Yes," Billy assured the hamster, "they were tucked in the back. In fact . . ."

He was about to explain how the notes, falling from the book, had saved the situation with Barrie Barns, but the hamster was hurrying ahead. "You see, Billy, that book has been in my family for generations but I was never able to understand any of it.

"Then, the other weekend, I had a remarkable stroke of good fortune. I was browsing around the car boot sale down at the old wharf – it's amazing what you can find at these things, Billy. That silver

plate on the mantelpiece, for instance, I picked that up at a car boot sale . . ."

Billy glanced at the plate. Real silver wasn't supposed to go rusty, was it?

But Mr Hammond, rambling on, somehow got back on to the right track before he could say anything. "Anyway, Billy, there I was at the sale and who should I see but Miss Bell, the music teacher. There she was with her little hatchback stuffed with all sorts of junk. Apparently her grandfather had left it all to her in his will."

Mr Hammond described how he had spent a happy hour delving through the treasures in Miss Bell's hatchback. An hour which ended with the triumphant discovery of a blue stone, covered in strange symbols.

"I recognized the symbols at once, Billy. They were the same as those in the book. But more than that. The stone held the key to the code. With the stone, I could read the book."

In a flash, Mr Hammond leapt down on to the book which Billy had picked up to examine. "You see the title, Billy?" The hamster skipped lightly over the odd symbols. "It's quite simple, once you know the code. It says, *The Practical Wizard's Do-It-Yourself Handbook.*"

For the next half hour, Billy sat, riveted as Mr Hammond described how, after translating some of the book, he had decided to try out one of the spells. He described the special mixture he made, into which he dipped a pencil to be used as a wand. Then he told of how the spell required the book to be buried in a tin box, at least two hundred paces away.

"And so, Billy, I was ready. Ready to turn Chips, my canary, into a hamster. I took the pencil – the wand, that is – and . . . but wait, I'm forgetting. I can show you all this. I filmed everything with the video camera."

Quickly, Mr Hammond explained to Billy how to take the tape from the camera and fit it into the video player, beneath the television set. The only problem Billy had was finding the television – it was behind another pile of books. At last they were ready.

"Draw the curtains, Billy, so that we can see better," Mr Hammond said. As

he pulled the curtains together, Billy thought he saw a movement outside but then shook his head. His imagination was working overtime.

The first picture that appeared on the screen was of a huge eye. "Ah, run it on a bit, Billy. That was where I'd got the camera the wrong way round," Mr Hammond said, apologetically. "There, stop it there."

The speeded-up picture slowed to normal pace as Billy pressed the button on the controller. The scene was the room in which they were sitting. In the centre of the picture was the bird cage containing Chips. From the speaker came the sound of footsteps and then a crash followed by a yell ("I fell over a pile of books," the hamster whispered to Billy) and then on to the screen staggered Mr Hammond. Mr Hammond as he used to be, that is. A plump, jolly sort of man wearing a knitted tie, a scruffy brown suit and glasses that dangled from a cord around his short neck.

"And now," the Mr Hammond on the screen announced, "I am ready to transform this canary into a hamster. Watch carefully. I have nothing up my sleeves, apart from my arms, of course. I point the specially prepared wand at the bird and recite the words PERENIKUM AD MILBA MOXI . . ."

As he pointed the wand at the canary, something dreadful happened. Chips, not liking the way Mr Hammond was pointing a pencil at him, shook his head violently. As he did so, he caught his little mirror which swung around. And as Mr Hammond uttered the last word, MOXI, the science master realized, too late, that the wand was pointing straight

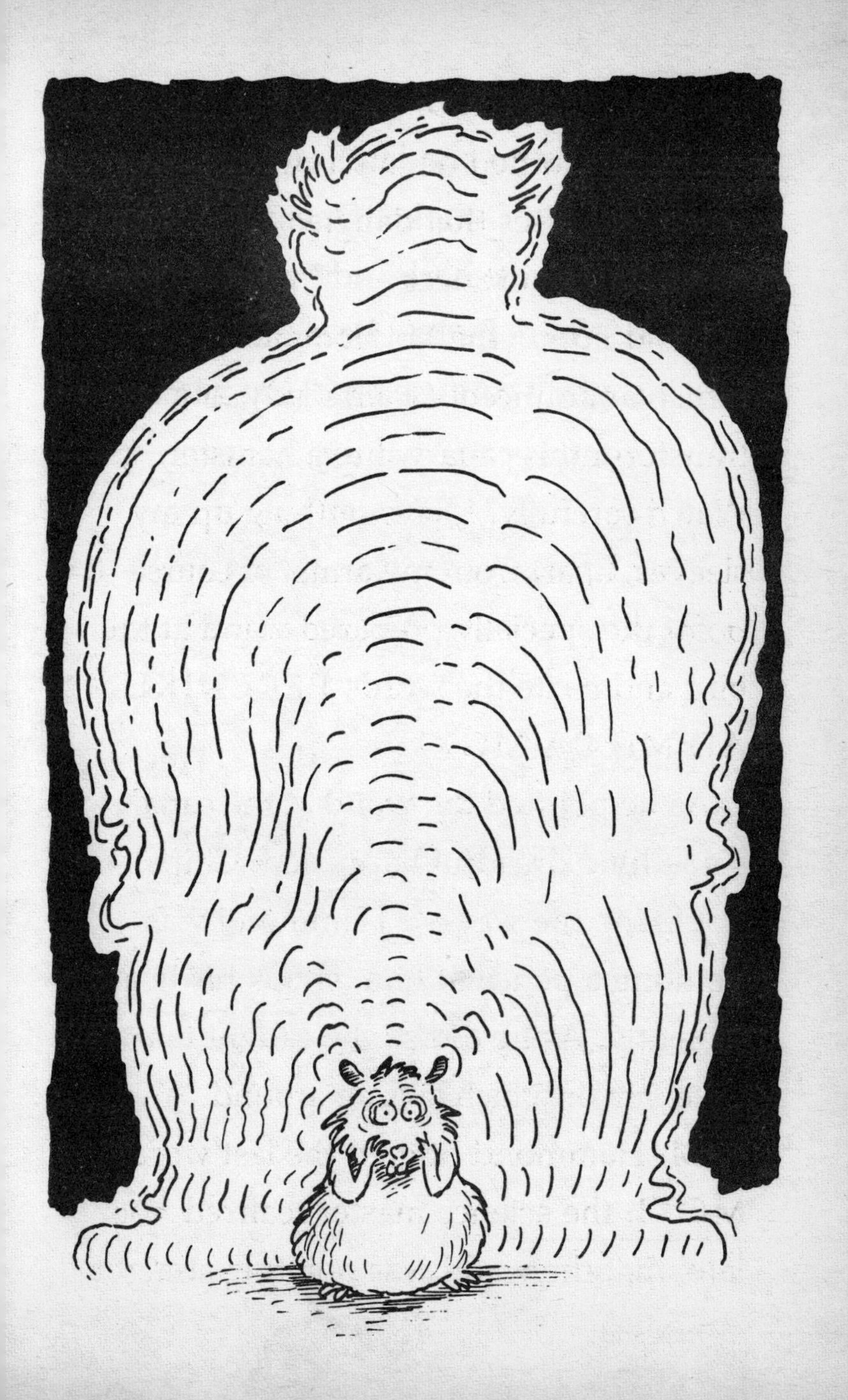

at his own reflection in the mirror.

There was no sudden flash. No magical puff of smoke. One moment Mr Hammond was there and the next he wasn't. Where he had been standing was just a slightly confused-looking hamster.

4
Nuts

Barrie Barns ducked, just as Billy came over to the window of The Old Boathouse to draw the curtains. Keeping low, he scrambled around to the back of the house where another boy, Nosy Wilkes, was waiting, keeping watch.

"What's he doing, then?" Nosy asked.

Barrie sat down beside Nosy, hunched up against the back wall of the house.

"He's nuts!" Barrie grinned. "Just sitting there talking to Old Hammy's hamster. No sign of Old Hammy, though. Funny thing. That hamster looks just like the one we found walking down the street last week and sold to old man Harris at the pet shop."

"How can you tell?" Nosy asked. "They all look the same to me."

"Dunno," Barrie replied, "just did, that's all."

"And did you see the book?"

"Yeah. The book was there all right. Good job you saw Beetle coming down here. I had to walk all the way down to school with old Ding Dong." He meant Miss Bell.

"What do you want it for anyway?" Nosy asked, living up to his nickname.

"Charity Day!" Barrie exclaimed. "Ding Dong asked me what I was planning to do to raise money for the Guide Dogs on Friday. I just said the first thing that came into my head. That book of Beetle's was really weird, I was still thinking about it. So, I told her that I'd got an old book written in ancient sort of writing and it was bound to be valuable so I'd sell raffle tickets for it on Friday."

"So, what are you going to do?"

"We'll wait here until Beetle comes out. Then, we'll grab him – and the book."

Inside the house, Billy had switched the television off and was talking to Mr Hammond again. The hamster was flicking through the notes that had been tucked into the back of the book.

"I must say," he said, struggling to read his own handwriting which looked even stranger than the symbols in the book, "it was a great stroke of luck that you came into the pet shop on Saturday."

"Oh, I always call in there on Saturdays to see Charlie. We have long chats, you know. He's a queer old bird."

"Really, Billy," Mr Hammond snapped, sounding like the schoolmaster he was. "Have respect for your elders, boy. You mustn't go around calling people, even pet shop owners, 'queer old birds'!"

Billy laughed. "No, I didn't mean Mr Harris. Charlie is the *parrot*."

Mr Hammond laughed, too. Only, as he was a hamster, it sounded more like a mouse with its tail trapped in a door. "Anyway, Billy," he said when he could finally stop squeaking, "did you have any difficulty finding the book where I'd buried it? It's lucky that I thought to

mark the place with a bit of driftwood."

"Just a small problem, Mr Hammond," Billy said. "You see, you buried it below the high-tide mark."

"Oh."

"Yes. The driftwood wasn't there any more. It's a good job you put it in the biscuit tin. It took me four hours, but I found it with my metal detector."

"Good boy. Remind me, when I'm

back to normal, and I'll see that your class teacher – Miss Roberts, isn't it – gives you an extra merit mark for initiative. Now then – ah – here we are." Mr Hammond seemed to have found what he was looking for amongst his notes.

"Yes." His tiny nose twitched along the scrawl that passed as Mr Hammond's handwriting. "It's pretty much as I remember it. To reverse the spell, I have to stand on the book at noon on the day before the next full moon – that's this Friday – and recite the magic words backwards."

"That's all right then," Billy said.

"There's just one small snag," Mr Hammond said, ominously. "Before the spell will work, I have to eat my own body weight of hazel-nuts."

Billy was puzzled. "That's not a snag," he said. "You must have done that already. That was a pound of nuts you've just eaten. You don't weigh anything like that much."

"You don't understand, Billy," Mr Hammond said. "Not my body weight as a *hamster*. My body weight as a *man*."

Billy gasped. Mr Hammond was not a tall man but he was very round.

"How much?" he whispered.

"Two hundred and ten pounds, Billy. I've got to eat two hundred and ten pounds of hazel-nuts before noon on Friday next."

"That's impossible," Billy gasped. "You'll have to wait until the next full moon."

"No good, Billy. It has to be done on the first full moon or not at all. If I can't do it before Friday I'll be a hamster for the rest of my life."

*

When they heard the door of Mr Hammond's house open, Barrie and Nosy crept around the side. When Billy appeared, he was only carrying his metal detector.

"Where's the book then?" Nosy hissed.

"Shhh! He's left it inside," Barrie said in what he fondly imagined was a whisper but was, in fact, loud enough to attract the attention of a deaf lady who was walking her dogs fifty yards away.

Billy didn't appear to hear him. His eyes stared out in front as though he was trying to work out a really weighty problem.

"Shall we grab him now then?" Nosy urged. On his own, Nosy wouldn't have had the nerve to grab a ham sandwich but, with Barrie there, he felt quite brave.

"Don't be stupid," Barrie rebuked him.

"There's no point in grabbing him, he hasn't got the book. Plan A is no good. We have to switch to Plan C."

Nosy was about to ask what had happened to Plan B but remembered, just in time, that the alphabet wasn't Barrie's best subject.

Unaware of his narrow escape, Billy walked slowly up the beach and back towards the town. He certainly did have a weighty problem. Two hundred and ten pounds of weighty problem. Well, two hundred and *nine* pounds, to be exact – Mr Hammond had already eaten one.

Whether or not a hamster can get through that amount of nuts in three-and-a-half days he would worry about later. The first thing was, where was he going to get them? Judging from how much that pound had cost, he was going to need about two years worth of pocket money and birthday money and he was flat broke.

He had money in the Savings Bank of course, but he needed his parents' signatures to get that out. He could imagine the conversation . . .

"Mum, Dad, can I draw some of my savings out?"

"What for, Billy?"

"I just fancy a few hazel-nuts."

"Can't you use your pocket money?"

"I've spent it."

"What? Already? You only had it this morning. Oh, all right, here's a pound, but you'll have to pay it back."

"Thanks, but I need a bit more than that."

"More? How many hazel-nuts do you want, Billy?"

"Two hundred and ten pounds."

"Whaaaa...?!"

"No, hang on, not that much."

"You had us going there, Billy."

"No, not two hundred and ten pounds. I meant two hundred and nine."

End of conversation.

Billy looked at his watch. It was a quarter to five. Something else caught his eye. A sign.

TONY'S TREASURE TROVE. WE BUY AND SELL ANYTHING. INSTANT CASH AVAILABLE.

He realized that he had reached Templebay's main shopping street and he was outside the junk shop. That's it!

He'd sell something. But what? He switched the metal detector from one hand to the other as he tried to think.

There was his plastic model of a Giant Woolly Mammoth but his mum had broken the trunk off while she was cleaning his room. She'd tried to mend it but, thinking it was the tail, she'd stuck it back on the wrong end.

What about his computer? No, no one would want that. It only had a 48K memory. Practically Stone Age.

Slowly his eyes went down to his hands and what was in them. No. He couldn't. Not his metal detector. No, not that. Absolutely not!

He went into the shop.

5
The Supermarket Snatcher

As soon as Billy was out of sight, Barrie and Nosy went around to the front of Mr Hammond's house and up the steps to the door. Barrie knocked loudly.

"I thought you said Old Hammy wasn't there?" Nosy said.

"I said I couldn't see him," Barrie replied. "Doesn't mean he isn't in." He knocked again. No reply.

"What now then?" Nosy asked.

"We go in and get the book. Got a bit of wire, Nosy?"

One of the reasons Barrie went around with Nosy was the incredible amount of junk that Nosy carried around in his pockets. Whatever you needed, you only had to ask Nosy. A pen-knife, a paper-clip, a half-chewed toffee-bar covered in fluff, these and many other wonders lurked in the dark, unfathomed depths of Nosy's pockets.

The other reason Barrie went around with Nosy, of course, was that Nosy was the only boy that would have anything to do with Barrie Barns.

Nosy fished in an inside pocket of his windcheater. "This do?" he asked, pulling out a wire coat-hanger. Caught on the hook were a bright green handkerchief, a Kit Kat wrapper, a paper tissue that Nosy had used to blot the orange juice that he'd spilled on his maths exercise book, and a long piece of string with a conker on the end.

"That's brilliant, Nosy," Barrie exclaimed, taking the coat-hanger from

his friend and pulling off the decorations. "Have you ever thought of going on the Paul Daniels Magic Show?"

Barrie untwisted the coat-hanger until he had the end free. He then bent the last half inch and, with Nosy keeping watch, poked it into the keyhole.

"I've seen them do this on the telly,"

he muttered as he fiddled with the wire. To Nosy's (and Barrie's) amazement, the lock suddenly clicked loudly. Barrie stood back.

"I've done it," he proclaimed. "Anybody about?"

"No. All clear," Nosy said, looking all around.

"Right then. In we go." Barrie gripped the door knob, twisted it and stepped forward.

Thud!

"Ouch!"

Barrie jumped back, clutching his nose which had collided with the door. The door was still closed. "You berk," Nosy exclaimed, forgetting for the moment who he was talking to. "The door wasn't locked in the first place. All you've done is lock it."

Luckily for Nosy, Barrie was so occupied with checking if his nose was still fixed to the front of his face that he missed the first couple of words.

Half an hour later, Barrie pulled the wire out of the keyhole. "It's no good," he said. "Must be one of those triple whatsit security locks. I can't budge it."

Both boys leaned back against the door and then slumped down until they were squatting there like a pair of unwanted bookends left out for the dustmen.

"What now?" Nosy mumbled.

"Let me think, let me think."

"Plan Z?" Nosy suggested.

*

As Billy stepped out of Tony's Treasure Trove, he saw the owner placing his precious metal detector in the front of the window. The price on it was twice the amount he had paid Billy for it. Billy groaned.

Still, he had sufficient money now to buy enough nuts to keep Mr Hammond going for tonight. He'd just have to think of something else tomorrow.

He reached the supermarket a few minutes later and, taking a trolley, made his way through the entrance. There was a notice-board just inside where people could advertise things on postcards. Useful things like:

BABY BUGGY AS NEW
ONLY NEEDS 3 NEW WHEELS

or

ASSORTED NAILS
ONLY USED ONCE
SLIGHTLY BENT

He scanned the postcards quickly, with the forlorn hope that he might find:

LARGE QUANTITY OF HAZEL-
NUTS FOR SALE
VERY CHEAP
UNWANTED GIFT

It was a forlorn hope, of course.

Then, his eye was drawn to the poster at the end of the notice-board. In large letters it said,

REWARD FOR
INFORMATION LEADING TO
THE ARREST OF THE
SUPERMARKET SNATCHER

Under this headline in smaller print, he read:

SHOP-EE-ZEE SUPERMARKETS OFFER A SUBSTANTIAL REWARD TO ANYONE WHO CAN HELP IDENTIFY THE MAN KNOWN AS THE SUPERMARKET SNATCHER. THIS MAN IS A MASTER OF DISGUISE AND HAS ESCAPED WITH LARGE AMOUNTS OF MONEY SNATCHED FROM THE TILLS OF VARIOUS BRANCHES OF SHOP-EE-ZEE SUPERMARKETS.

A substantial reward. That's what he could do with. Billy decided to keep a very careful eye open as he pushed his trolley around the aisles.

Inside, since it was November, the Christmas decorations were starting to look a little tatty as they had been up so long. The tinsel on the Easter Egg display looked particularly limp and the background music was decidedly wobbly (Ru–oo–dolf the–er–er–er re–we–we–

wedno–wo–wo–wosed reinde–yer–yer–yer . . .).

Billy set off down the first aisle. He liked supermarket trolleys. Working up a good speed, he leaned forward, took his weight on his arms and lifted his feet from the ground. He must have found the only trolley in the place that ran in a straight line and he coasted happily past soap powders, washing-up liquids and bleach. He would have gone right past toothpaste and assorted toiletries on the one push if he hadn't had to make an emergency stop to avoid a vicar who was trying to decide what brand of after-shave to buy. He must have been getting it for a friend, since he had a short black beard.

Once past the vicar, Billy steered the trolley around the corner and prepared for another run. It was then he saw the scruffily dressed man wearing odd shoes. He, too, had a beard, but it was long, white and straggly. The man's trolley had a couple of cheap items in it but, as Billy watched, he reached out and took a tin of beef stew from the rack and shoved it quickly into his pocket.

Billy gasped. Could this be the Snatcher? His beard was obviously false,

but Billy decided not to rush up and pull it for the moment. He would just follow the man.

In the next ten minutes, Billy watched the man put one tin of tuna into his trolley and four cans of spaghetti hoops, a bottle of tomato ketchup (Giant Economy Size) and a bag of frozen chips into his pockets.

Goodness, Billy thought. He must

have deeper pockets than Nosy Wilkes. Just then, Billy realized he was passing the Christmas nuts display. Quickly, he scooped as many bags of hazel-nuts as he could afford into his trolley and then looked around to see where the man was. He had completely disappeared.

6
A Substantial Reward

Billy groaned. A quick search proved fruitless, and he decided the best thing to do was to go down to the check-out nearest to the entrance, pay for his nuts and hang around there to see if he could spot the man again.

"Good gracious, dear. Where do you live? The zoo?" The check-out lady looked aghast at the piles of hazel-nuts that Billy had placed by her till.

"Er, no. They're for my pet monkey," Billy said.

"What's his name, King Kong?" the lady asked. Billy decided to keep his mouth shut. He paid for the nuts and then waited by the entrance, looking for the man.

BING-BONG! The wobbly background music stopped and a bored lady's voice announced over the public address system, "Shop-ee-zee Supermarkets proudly present this week's special seasonal offers. Jolly Yuletide Baked Beans 2p off. Party Time Smoked Kippers, 10p off. Happy Holiday Toilet Rolls, 15p off." And then, finally, "Here, Doris, how do I switch this bloomin' microphone off?"

Billy and the rest of the shoppers in the supermarket would never know whether Doris could tell her how to switch the microphone off for, at that moment, a cry went up from one of the tills.

"Stop that man!" At the same moment, Billy spotted the scruffy man. He had passed through the check-outs and was headed towards him. As the cry

went up, the man glanced guiltily over his shoulder and then, leaving his trolley behind, took to his heels. The vicar must have seen him, too, for he was racing in pursuit.

Billy was ready. Just as the old man was about to pass him, he pushed the trolley with all his strength.

Unfortunately, this time it did not run straight. A wheel jammed and it spun in a circle. Even so, the man caught it a glancing blow and went sprawling with a clattering and smashing of the cans and bottles in his pockets on to the ground.

The trolley tipped and the bags of nuts

fell out, bursting as they hit the floor. The poor vicar tried to slow down, and managed to swerve around the overturned trolley. But then he put his heel down in the middle of the spilled nuts. His feet went from under him and he, too, went sprawling, shouting a word that Billy had never heard a vicar say before.

Pandemonium broke loose then, with security guards pouring in from all directions. Billy felt a hand on his arm. A big man with a very official look.

"I think you'd better come with me, son," he said.

A few minutes later, Billy found himself in the manager's office. The

manager, the man who had taken Billy's arm, was sitting at his desk with the telephone to his ear. Billy sat in a comfortable chair, opposite.

The manager put the phone down. "Well, now, son – er, what's your name?"

"Billy. Billy Lowe."

"Well, Billy, it seems we have you to thank for the capture of the Supermarket Snatcher. Well done."

"It *was* him, then?" Billy said, hardly able to believe it. "I thought it was. I thought as soon as I saw him that that beard was false. It was false, wasn't it?"

"Oh, it was false, all right," the manager smiled.

"Yes, well, I could tell. It was a bit too white and straggly."

"White?"The manager looked puzzled and then realization dawned. "Ah, you mean the scruffy fellow. The one with all the stuff in his pockets. No, no. that's just old Arthur. He often pops in around this time of year for a bit of shop-lifting. We usually pick him up quietly, outside. No, old Arthur isn't the Snatcher. The Snatcher was the fellow with the *black* beard. The one dressed as a vicar."

Billy was stunned. For a while he didn't hear what the manager was saying but then his ears picked up the word "reward" and he pulled himself together again.

". . . and so, if you'll tell me where you live, I shall come around personally with the cheque, Billy."

"Er . . . h–how much did you s–say?" Billy stammered.

The manager told him. Billy sat, silent for a moment. Then, a little nervously, he asked, "Could I have the reward in goods instead of cash?"

The manager considered and then said, "I don't see why not. What did you have in mind?" Billy took a deep breath.

"Would two hundred and nine pounds of hazel-nuts be all right?"

To the manager's credit, he didn't bat an eyelid. He'd been a supermarket manager a long time and had encountered a lot of remarkable things. After just a moment's hesitation, he looked back at Billy and said, "Of course. Will you eat them here or shall we deliver?"

Billy would have liked to have gone back to Mr Hammond's house to give him the good news but time was getting on and his parents would be wondering where he had got to. He managed to persuade the manager that he really didn't want his picture in the local newspaper and went straight home from the supermarket. The nuts would be delivered to The Old Boathouse at five o'clock the following evening, and Billy would be there to receive them.

And so it was that he didn't receive the terrible news until he called in, on his way to school, the next morning.

"It was those two rascals, Barrie Barns and Nosy Wilkes, the same two that found me when I was trying to get to school and sold me to Pets' Paradise," Mr Hammond told a shocked Billy.

"I could hear someone messing about with the lock after you'd left. Somehow, the idiots managed to lock a door that was unlocked in the first place and they obviously didn't know about the spare key on the hook under the steps."

Billy nodded. "That's the first place I looked," he said. "I wondered how you managed to lock it, you being . . ."

"Yes, yes," Mr Hammond interrupted, impatiently. "Anyway, I thought they'd given up and gone away, but then they smashed the window and came in that way."

"And they just took the book, sir? Nothing else?" Billy asked.

"*Just* the book?! Billy, without the book the spell won't work! We have to get it back, Billy. I'll start on the nuts as soon as they arrive, tonight. But we must get that book back by Friday noon."

7

A Hitch in Time

Billy couldn't face his breakfast. It was Friday. The whole week had gone by and he still hadn't come up with a plan to get the book back.

"Come on, Billy, eat your breakfast," his mother urged him. But he just couldn't.

He got up from his chair, suddenly, and headed for the door.

"Now where are you off to?" His father looked up from the cornflakes packet he had been reading.

"School, Dad. It's Charity Day and I want to get in early."

Fifteen minutes later, he was climbing the wooden steps of The Old Boathouse.

Pushing the door open, he was greeted by the usual chaos – plus more! Now, the books which lay everywhere were themselves covered. By a layer of hazel-nut shells.

On the table squatted the unhappy hamster. He had definitely grown since yesterday, Billy thought. He shuddered to think how many of the

nuts Mr Hammond had eaten.

"Hello, Billy," Mr Hammond said. "Any luck?" Billy shook his head.

"All we can do is wait and see if Barrie brings the book into school today. He's been bragging about it."

"Yes, well, if he does, that might provide us with a chance," Mr Hammond said, thoughtfully. "I'm coming in with you this morning, Billy. I can't look another hazel-nut in the face. He waved a paw in the direction of the still uneaten bags of nuts. "I think I've managed to get through about two thirds of them and that's just going to have to be enough."

Half past eleven. Billy sat at his desk in the classroom. Tucked into his top pocket was Mr Hammond. All was not lost, he could see the book on Barrie

Barns' desk over the other side of the room.

Miss Roberts, Billy's teacher was talking to a girl in a blue check dress, at the front of the class.

"Thank you, Rebecca," she was saying. "I'm sure your sponsored skip will earn a lot of money for the Guide Dogs. And don't worry, just because Elaine and Emma had the same idea."

Rebecca went back to her desk and Miss Roberts addressed the class.

"Right, then, girls and boys. We're doing very well so far. Three sponsored skips, a sponsored headstand and Nosy, er, I mean, Norman Wilkes is going to try to remain silent for a whole day. Now then, who's going to be next? Billy? What are you going to do?"

Billy was staring into space thinking about the book. He was suddenly aware that everyone was looking at him.

"Um . . . sorry, Miss Roberts?"

"I asked you, Billy, what you are planning to do for Charity Day."

Billy was horrified. With all the worries about Mr Hammond, he had completely forgotten that he was supposed to be doing something for the Guide Dogs. He began to panic but then he had a sudden inspiration.

"Ah, I'm going to sell tickets to a show starring my performing educated hamster."

The whole class roared with laughter. Mr Hammond was not amused though. "How can you do this to me, Billy?" he hissed.

But Billy was already on his feet and walking to the front of the class. For the next ten minutes, Mr Hammond amazed everyone. With the help of some marbles

which Miss Roberts had confiscated from Barrie Barns, he correctly gave the answers to the sums that Billy wrote on the board. He went on to find the capitals of a dozen countries on Miss Roberts' world map, which Billy spread on the floor. Then, just to finish things

off, he did a triple back somersault and bowed to the class.

Billy went back to his seat to loud cheers from the class. Miss Roberts looked a little dazed.

"Most unusual, most unusual. You must show your extraordinary hamster to Mr Hammond when he comes back. Now then."

She began to recover her composure and continued, brightly, "As they say in show business, follow that! Barrie Barns. What are you going to contribute to the cause?"

Barrie stood up and, picking up the book, walked out to the front of the class.

Billy glanced quickly at the clock. Five to twelve! He had to do something in the next five minutes.

Barrie was in front of Miss Roberts. He

was offering the book to her. He seemed to be holding it for a long time. Miss Roberts didn't move. Billy looked around. *Nobody* was moving. Even the second hand on the clock had stopped moving. Something really weird was going on.

Every girl, every boy in the class was frozen in position. Emma was leaning over towards her best friend, Sara, her mouth frozen open, her whisper suspended on her motionless lips. Incredibly, the paper dart which Nosy had just thrown hung unsupported in the air.

Billy got up. At least *he* could move. He went over to the window and looked out into the street. The same thing. Cars, shoppers, birds, everything was frozen in mid-movement. He took Mr Hammond from his pocket.

"That's terrific," he said. "How did you do it without the book?"

"It wasn't me, Billy," Mr Hammond said. "It wasn't one of *my* spells."

"But . . ."

Then, the door opened. "Hello, Billy. Hello, Mr Hammond."

"Miss Bell!" Billy exclaimed. "How come . . . I mean, how do you know. . . ?"

"Oh, I know lots of things, Billy. It's my job. And I don't mean music teaching. Let's say I'm here to keep an eye on things. Magical things."

"You mean *you* did this?" Billy swept his arm around the still classroom.

"Well, I had to do something, didn't I? We can't have Mr Hammond spending the rest of his life as a hamster, can we?"

Miss Bell went over to the motionless Barrie Barns and took the book from his hand. "You'd better give Mr Hammond to me," she said. "I'll take him to the staff room, it's empty at the moment. Go back to your desk, Billy, I shall start things moving again as soon as I get there. Mr Hammond will just have time to reverse his spell."

Billy gave Mr Hammond, who still hadn't said a word, to Miss Bell, and headed back to his desk. Then he stopped.

"Miss Bell," he asked. "When you start things moving again, will they know that anything has happened?"

"Of course not, Billy. Nothing has

happened for them. Apart from the book, of course. Barrie will be rather surprised to see that it has vanished."

"Then I've got an idea, Miss," Billy said. He went to Barrie's desk and, taking out an exercise book, ripped a page from it. With Barrie's pen, he wrote something, in a fair copy of Barrie's awful writing, folded the paper and placed it in his hand. The hand which had been holding the book.

Winking at Miss Bell, he then went back to his desk and waited.

Shortly after Miss Bell had left the room, everything started to move again.

Miss Roberts blinked. She could have sworn that Barrie was offering her a book. Now, she could see, it was just a piece of paper. Barrie was just as surprised.

He was even more surprised, a

moment later, when a beaming Miss Roberts read the note out to the class:

I, Barrie Barns, pledge all of my pocket money for a whole year to the Guide Dogs Fund.

Barrie couldn't believe his ears. Before he could say anything, Miss Roberts was talking to him.

"Barrie Barns," she said. "Of all people! This is *most* generous. Class, three cheers for Barrie Barns!"

Barrie was flabbergasted. Everyone cheered, especially Billy. Barrie had never been cheered before. He liked it!

"What's all this noise then?" No one had heard the door open. Into the room strode – Mr Hammond! The *real* Mr Hammond, not the hamster. Billy looked at the clock. Just gone noon.

"Mr Hammond, you're back!" Miss Roberts exclaimed. "But look at you. So slim. You've lost pounds."

Billy remembered that Mr Hammond hadn't been able to finish the nuts.

"Ah, yes, Miss Roberts," Mr Hammond said. "I've been away. On a special diet. A very special diet."

"Oh, but Mr Hammond," a little girl's voice piped up. "If you're on a diet, does that mean you won't be buying a slice of the cake I baked specially for Charity Day?"

"Well, now, Sara," Mr Hammond chuckled. "I'm sure I can make an exception in that case. What is it?"

"Hazel-nut cake, sir."

Mr Hammond fainted.

And so Mr Hammond resumed normal life at Templebay Junior, Billy got three

merit marks and Miss Bell would wink at him and put her finger to her lips whenever they met.

But, this story has another happy ending. Barrie Barns, whose only friend in the world until recently had been

Nosy Wilkes, suddenly found he had lots of them. He discovered, in fact, that it was nice being nice. He helped Billy and Mr Hammond replace the broken window at The Old Boathouse and began a friendship with the smaller boy that was to grow stronger and stronger. He even stopped calling Billy "Beetle" and gave him his metal detector.

And Miss Bell? She's still there, of course. Just keeping her eye on things.